For Sophie, the life-saver

www.dragonbloodpirates.co.uk

ORCHARD BOOKS
338 Euston Road, London NW1 3BH

First published in 2008 by Lothian Children's Books,
an imprint of Hachette Livre Australia
First published in the UK in 2011 by Orchard Books

ISBN 978 1 40830 828 8

10 9 8 7 6 5 4 3 2 1

Printed in Great Britain

Orchard Books is a division of Hachette Children's Books,
an Hachette UK company.

www.hachette.co.uk

Dragon Blood Pirates

The Power of the Scabbard

Dan Jerris

ORCHARD BOOKS

Death Isl

Shipwreck Island.

Cannibal Island

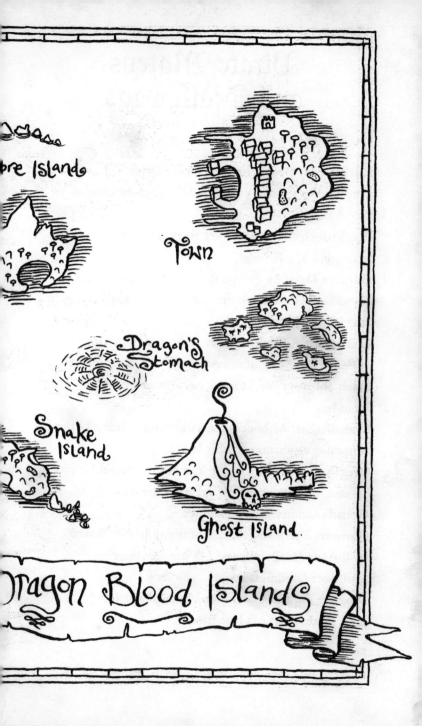

Pirate Mateys and Scallywags

Alleric (Al) Breas: Lives in Drake Drive and owns a mysterious sea trunk that takes him to the Dragon Blood Islands

Blacktooth McGee: A very nasty pirate who runs the brigantine *The Revenge*

Demon Dan: An evil pirate who died on Dragon Island and whose black diamond became stuck between a dragon's teeth

Evil Pearl: A deathless pirate who becomes Queen of Pearl Island and sacrifices people to a sea monster

Flash Johnny: Blacktooth's devious and greedy cabin boy

Grandfather: Mahoot's grandfather and guardian of the swimming elephants on Sabre Island

Greeny Joe: A shark so big and old that mould grows on his skin, making him glow green in the dark

Grenda: Snotty Nell's daughter

Gunner: The pirate captain of the ship *The Invincible*

Halimeda (Hally) Breas: Al's younger sister

Mahoot: Captain Gunner's cabin boy

Mozzy: *The Invincible*'s bosun – small and fast

Jack Seabrook: Al's best friend

Pigface McNurt: Blacktooth's bosun; a huge pirate with a ring through his nose

Prince Alleric: The prince who once ruled Sabre Island but disappeared in mysterious circumstances

Princess Haree: The princess of Ruby Island

Razor Toe: A deathless pirate who has enslaved the people of Ruby Island

Sharkbait: Snotty Nell's one-legged bosun

Slicer: *The Invincible*'s cook

Snakeboot: A magical white three-legged cat with purple eyes. Legend has it he once belonged to a terrifying pirate called Vicious Victor.

Snotty Nell: A horrible one-eyed pirate who sails a worn-out Indiaman called *Nausi VIII*

Stanley Spong: A crooked, sneaky trader in town who cheats people

Vampire Zu: Snotty Nell's huge first mate

Velvetfoot: A fearsome pirate distinctive for his velvet shoes that let him creep up on his victims unannounced

Vicious Victor: A pirate ghost. He used to pillage the Dragon Blood Islands and stole the magical sabre and scabbard that belonged to Prince Alleric.

Invincible

Alleric Breas had just finished polishing the Scabbard of Invincibility when his best friend, Jack Seabrook, bounced happily into the attic. Al held the scabbard up to show Jack — its four black diamonds glittered on the silver mesh.

Jack picked up the Dragon Blood Sabre, which was beside Al, and swished it through the air. "Wow! Don't they both look great?" he said.

Snakeboot, their white, three-legged cat,

purred loudly in approval from the lid of an old sea trunk.

Jack reached out to touch the scabbard. "Does it work?"

Al shrugged. "I wouldn't like to test it. To do that I'd have to try and injure myself."

"But we could try something easy," suggested Jack. "I could stick a pin in your finger and see if it makes a mark."

Al reached into a cupboard drawer, rummaged around, found a pin and held it out. Jack gave Al's hand a quick jab. To his surprise the pin bent, and Al's finger was untouched.

"Wow!" the boys said together. Then they rushed downstairs to the bathroom, ran the hot tap and Al stuck his finger under it. He didn't feel the hot water at all. "It works," he chortled. "It really works! I'm invincible!"

They returned to the attic where Snakeboot leapt from the trunk. He sunk his claws into Al's arm.

"Not a scratch," smiled Al, reaching down
to pat the cat. "Thanks, Snakeboot."

Snakeboot purred and leapt back onto the
trunk, but this time he clawed the lid. "Are
you saying it's time to go?" asked Jack.

"We'd better change into our pirate clothes," said Al. "This time I hope we land on Sabre Island so we can show Mahoot's grandfather that we've got the scabbard working."

Minutes later the boys were dressed and eagerly following Snakeboot into Al's grandfather's sea trunk. Al focused on the map of the Dragon Blood Islands drawn in the bottom, and especially on Sabre Island. As he wished himself there, his arms and legs began to tingle. He saw his friend Jack began to shimmer and dissolve, and both boys left number five Drake Drive and the twenty-first century.

Cobra

Al and Jack found themselves in a familiar pergola. "We're in the summer house on Sabre Island," said Al, looking around. He opened a creaky old door and stepped outside into a bird-filled jungle.

As they made their way down to a nearby creek, voices carried to the boys through the trees. "Put your backs into it! I've got two hogsheads to fill by tonight's tide."

"That's Mozzy bossing the crew around," said Al, quickening his pace, with Snakeboot bounding behind him.

They soon came across *The Invincible*'s crew filling water barrels in the sun. Captain Gunner was sitting in the shade of a large tree and, seeing the boys, leapt to his feet.

"You're back!" he cried. "And you've brought Snakeboot, too. We've missed him!"

A bare-footed boy turned and rushed towards his friends.

"Mahoot!" said Al and Jack together.

"You've repaired the scabbard," said Gunner, eyeing the glittering weapon. "That's great. I'm sure we're gunner get lots of treasure now!"

Jack laughed. Gunner's first thought was always of treasure. "Before we go treasure hunting," he said, "we want to see Mahoot's grandfather."

"He'll be so happy," said Mahoot. "He still dreams of Sabre Island being a safe place again."

"Why don't we sit down for a few minutes before you rush off?" suggested Gunner. "I'd love to look at your treasures. You can tell me how you got the sabre working again and how it brought you here."

Al and Jack sat down with Gunner under the tree. "We haven't actually got the sabre working," Jack tried to explain. "If Al had managed that, how could he have got Snakeboot and me here too? There's other magic happening and we just haven't worked it out properly yet."

"Well," said Gunner, "I can understand you don't want folk believing the sabre's working." He touched his nose and winked. "But you can trust me. I'll tell everyone else it's not working. I was just hoping you were gunner tell me the—"

His words were interrupted by a growl from Snakeboot. The cat's fur stood on end, his back arched threateningly and his purple eyes glared at something next to Gunner.

A large cobra reared from the bushes, its hood flaring, poised and ready to strike. Behind it several smaller cobras squirmed aggressively.

"It's a nest!" shouted Jack. "We're sitting on a cobra's nest!"

"Don't move!" cried Al. But his warning was of no use because Gunner, seeing the snake, let out a yell and leapt away. Unfortunately, his feet tangled, making him fall, and his frantic movements attracted the cobras.

Without thinking, Al threw himself between Gunner and the snakes just as they slithered forward. Covered in cobras, Al rolled on the ground. The smaller snakes clung to his jacket and wrapped around his legs, while the large one struck at his neck. Finally, Al stopped moving and sat up, slightly stunned, with the snakes writhing angrily

around him. Poison dripped from his jacket
and breeches, but not a drop had gone into
his skin. Ashen-faced, he pulled the snakes
off and threw them into the jungle. The crew
of *The Invincible* stood around him, staring in
awe.

"The scabbard has saved you," said
Gunner. "And you saved me!"

"That's amazing," said Slicer, the cook. "If
I hadn't seen it, I'd not believe it!"

"It really works!" cried Mahoot. "This is
the best news ever!"

But as Al looked around at his friends, he

wasn't so sure. Gunner's eyes flashed with jealousy and Slicer's gaze was greedy. *I must remember they're pirates*, he thought, but then he shook the idea away. Gunner was his friend, after all, and there was a pirate code! Al was sure he was safe with his shipmates.

Later that night, the boys sat around Mahoot's grandfather's table and, after they had enjoyed a delicious meal of saffron rice and jungle vegetables, Al put the sabre and scabbard on the table for the old man to see.

Strangely, Mahoot's grandfather didn't touch them. He looked at Al sadly.

"Now, young Prince Alleric," he said, "thank you for finding these treasures and offering them to me. Unfortunately I cannot take them yet. Despite all your hard work, the magical words that give the sabre its strength have not yet been found. Without those words you cannot come and go as

you please. I am old, but I know I will live
till you find those words and restore the
sabre's powers. Until then, you must keep
these weapons and continue your search.
With their return, however, dangerous times
begin for you. Every man will want them.
Remember to keep one eye open, even
when you sleep. There are perils outside the
jungle and there is a poison in men's hearts
that causes more damage than any snake."

The Lure of Treasure

After a day on Sabre Island, where they swam with the elephants and visited the elephant's graveyard with Mahoot's grandfather, Al and Jack set sail with Gunner at sunset and headed for town.

The following day Gunner went ashore to spy on other captains' sailing plans and what they might be carrying. "There might be a load of silk we can steal, or a hold of spices," he said to Mozzy, the bosun. "There have been very few pickings leaving town lately."

Left alone, Al, Jack and Mahoot enjoyed watching the hustle and bustle of the crowded port from the decks of *The Invincible*, until Gunner returned later in the afternoon and called them over.

"I've got an errand for you," he said. "My compass is broken." He handed Al some gold pieces. "I'd like you to go over to Stanley Spong's and buy a good second-hand one."

As the boys and Snakeboot went to disembark, Gunner called out, "I wouldn't take the sabre and scabbard with you. You'll be robbed!"

"He's right," agreed Jack. "Put them in our cabin. We won't be long."

An hour later, carrying a brass compass and feeling pleased that they had got the best possible price from Spong, the boys returned to the docks. Snakeboot bounded ahead, but as they approached the wharf where *The Invincible* had berthed, they found it empty.

"Have we got the wrong quay?" asked Jack, bewildered.

"Snakeboot never makes mistakes," said Al, staring uncomfortably at the empty mooring lines rolled neatly on the jetty.

"Then Gunner's gone without us," said Mahoot, disbelieving. "Unless his ship was hijacked."

"What will we do?" said Jack. "We've got nowhere to stay."

"But more importantly, where on earth has it gone and how will we find it?" asked Al, shocked.

What the boys didn't know was that Gunner had returned from town with some very interesting news. Blacktooth was back!
The gossip was that he had recently rowed into town in a patched-up longboat. He had brought with him a casket of gold and purchased a well-found barque which he had renamed *The Tyrant*. He'd fitted it out with ten cannons and set sail. It was rumoured that he was planning to return to buy another ship, load it with timber and build a fort on some secret island.

The news was too much for Gunner. He knew which island Blacktooth was living on and how he had ended up with the treasure of Velvetfoot, the deathless pirate. That treasure, he told himself, should have been his. If it hadn't been for those children making a deal with Blacktooth's cabin boy, Flash, then the treasure would be sitting in Gunner's hold.

I'm gunner attack Blacktooth and take his gold as he sails into town, thought Gunner as he made his way back to his ship. *I'm gunner sail this afternoon and wait for him near that group of small islands I know about. I'll spring out with all guns firing.* The Invincible's *got*  long-range cannons, *so he's got no chance. But we'll have to board* The Tyrant *and Blacktooth's a dirty fighter. If I had the Scabbard of Invincibility I'd beat him in a second!*

Once back on *The Invincible*, Gunner went to his cabin and brooded. He knew the boys wouldn't let him have the scabbard. But, if they weren't around, and the scabbard was just lying in their cabin…

And before he knew what he was doing, Gunner had left the boys on their errand and set sail without them.

War of Words

Gunner sailed to a group of small islands that lay beside a fast current the merchantmen used to navigate into town. There was only one safe anchorage and it was very small, but it hid any ship from sight. It was the perfect place to launch an attack on a passing vessel. All Gunner had to do was set a watch on the headland and, when the signal was given that Blacktooth's barque was sighted, set sail into the current and cut him off.

As dusk fell, Gunner, with the last of

the wind, forced *The Invincible* against the current and slid into the anchorage. To his horror, a worn-out old West Indiaman was already moored in his spot. "It's Snotty!" he grumbled. "What's she doing here? Could she have found out about Blacktooth's treasure and be setting an ambush too?"

Meanwhile, Snotty Nell and her daughter, Grenda, were sitting on the poop deck of the *Nausi VIII*, and Snotty was enjoying her favourite drink, sahlep tea. She was doing her best, as usual, not to look over the side of the boat into the water, because circling below was a huge white pointer shark, Greeny Joe.

Snotty's nerves were on edge. Her temper was raw and unsettled and she was very worried. Her first mate, Vampire Zu, had just given her some bad news.

She sipped her tea and sighed. "Now, Grenda, I don't want to worry you, but

we've got Toledo worms in the hull. The old *Nausi VIII* could sink any day. I've brought us here because this is a good spot to hunt for a new boat, and we're sheltered from storms. If we're lucky, a slow merchantman might sail past us tomorrow, and we can swap boats with the captain." She sighed again. "Hopefully without too much of a struggle."

Snotty was interrupted by the arrival of

The Invincible. She leapt to her feet in surprise and watched as Gunner set anchor, too close for comfort.

His voice floated over the water. "Snotty, you old witch! You've got no hope! The treasure's mine!"

"What treasure?" muttered Snotty. "What is he going on about?" She cupped her hands to her mouth and yelled, "I can beat you to any treasure, you pox-faced blowfish!"

Gunner raced to the bow and shook his fist at her. "Your stinking slow old boat will never beat Blacktooth's barque! Give up now, you sorry jellyfish!"

In the setting sun, something glittered brightly from Gunner's waist. Snotty grabbed her spyglass and focused. Instantly she saw the Scabbard of Invincibility and the Dragon Blood Sabre. A smile came over her face and her good eye gleamed at the sight of a treasure she could steal, if she played her cards right. She turned to Grenda.

"I think our Captain Gunner has taken something he shouldn't have," she said. "Would your mates, Al and Jack, have given him their sabre and scabbard?" She handed the spyglass to Grenda.

Grenda gasped at the sight of Gunner wearing the legendary weapons. "I don't think they would have," she replied. "He must have stolen them."

Snotty laughed. "They're worth a fortune. Spong could sell them for more than the price of a new boat." She turned and shook her fist at Gunner. "I don't give up!" she screamed. "In fact, I'll get the treasure and I'll rip yer heart out and dance to its beat!"

In answer, Gunner fired a cannon. The shot fell slightly short of the bow and landed in the sea.

As the sun sank in the sky and clouds rolled in, dimming the starlight, Snotty smiled. She doused all lights on board the *Nausi VIII*.

At midnight, when Snotty was sure Gunner would have set watch and gone to bed, she launched the longboat, filled it with heavily armed men, and sent them off to row silently towards *The Invincible*.

On board Gunner's ship, Mozzy was on watch. He kept his spyglass fixed on Snotty's boat, and even in the gloomy light he thought he could see movement. Minutes later, his sharp ears caught the sound of muffled rowing. He raced below and shook Gunner awake. "Snotty's about to attack!" he cried.

Gunner leapt out of bed, hurriedly pulling on his pants. "Rouse the men and arm them," he ordered as he grabbed his coat. He rushed from his cabin and ran to the stern, where he put the spyglass to work and soon

spotted the longboat. "Snotty's getting soft in the brain if she thinks she can steal another boat from me," he grumbled.

Gunner and his men trained all their eyes on their target, waiting for Snotty's men to try to board near the bow. Suddenly, the longboat shifted direction and began to row towards the shore.

"What's going on?" muttered Gunner, straining to see properly in the gloom. "Is she planning some trap for the morning?" He ran the spyglass over the *Nausi VIII*. "She's up to something, and she thinks we can't see her. Don't lose sight of those men in the longboat! Maybe they're moving cannons to the shore and they'll fire on us from there."

Gunner kept worrying while the longboat rowed in a large circle and finally went back to the *Nausi VIII*, unaware that while he and his crew had been watching from the bow, a tiny dinghy had left the *Nausi VIII* and rowed quietly towards his ship from the opposite direction. It came silently under the prow. The rower hurled a light grappling hook, which caught onto *The Invincible*'s rails with barely a thump.

Then, hand over hand, a small figure shinnied up, slid over the rails and down through the hatchway, stole into Gunner's cabin and found the sabre and scabbard lying on the captain's desk.

The small thief quickly picked up the treasures and strapped them to her waist, then tiptoed out of the cabin and back the way she had come. Back on board the *Nausi VIII*, Grenda proudly handed the treasures to her mother.

Snotty waited until the longboat returned, then slipped anchor and drifted away, letting the current take her.

Gunner was puzzled when he saw the longboat being hauled on board the *Nausi VIII*. Then, as Snotty pulled anchor, he scratched his head and smiled. "They realised we were onto them."

"She's given up and she's leaving," agreed Mozzy.

"Aha!" laughed Gunner. "Looooser!" he shouted. "You're such a disgusting old pig that I don't even know why Greeny Joe wants to eat you!"

The men on Gunner's boat fell about laughing at Gunner's insult.

The Auction

Back in town, Al, Jack and Mahoot spent their first night back in the Dragon Blood Islands sleeping on the floor of the empty Alleric Warehouse, while Snakeboot busied himself hunting for rats. Eventually, hungry and increasingly unhappy, they took Captain Gunner's compass back to Spong's second-hand shop and sold it for a loss.

With the few coins Spong gave them, they bought themselves food and hung around the docks, hoping to see *The Invincible*'s sails or hear some news.

A few days later, with Snakeboot trotting at their side, they almost bumped into Snotty Nell as she strode down the wharf. She was dragging Grenda along by the hand and Vampire Zu was walking ahead, carrying a parcel wrapped in cloth.

Jack ran across to Grenda's side, but before he could say anything, Snotty growled, "Get away from here. I don't want you bilge rats anywhere near us!"

Jack took a step back, offended.

"After everything we've done for her," said Al, as Snotty carried on without breaking her stride.

Grenda turned her head, smiled, held up one hand and dropped something. It was so small that Al missed seeing it fall, but Mahoot dashed to get it before a passerby trod on it.

Mahoot unwrapped a small note with a picture of a flag:

"She's trying to tell us they're carrying dangerous goods," said Jack, who had recently studied maritime flags.

"What can she mean?" asked Mahoot.

"Grenda obviously had that note ready in case she saw us," said Al. "I think we should find out what Vampire Zu is carrying."

The boys raced after them and watched as Snotty, Vampire Zu and Grenda went into Spong's shop. Half an hour later they emerged, just as Stanley Spong placed a large cardboard sign in the window:

Stanley Spong's Emporium
is pleased to announce
the auction of the legendary
Dragon Blood Sabre
and Scabbard of Invincibility
Wednesday at the tenth hour
in the town square

"How on earth did they get them from Gunner?" asked Al, both horrified and annoyed.

"We know where they are now," said Mahoot, "and that's what counts. How will we get them back?"

"We should go in and tell Spong they were stolen from us," said Jack. "We should demand them back."

"But how can we even prove they belong to us?" asked Al. "And Spong wouldn't care anyway."

"What else can we do?" said Mahoot. "We haven't got any money."

As if in answer, Snakeboot clawed at his leg and let out a loud meow. Then he took off and ran through the streets.

The boys followed as Snakeboot led them back to the Alleric Warehouse. He raced through the giant storeroom, up some rickety stairs and into one of the old office rooms. "There's nothing in here, Snakeboot," said Mahoot, looking around the dusty, cobwebby room. "Why have you brought us up here?"

The cat meowed again and circled.

"Last time he brought us into an empty room, we found a secret cupboard using your elephant-head ring," Al said to Mahoot. "Then we found a treasure map."

The boys needed no further prompting and, trusting their clever cat, they began searching the walls looking for any sort of hidden door or cupboard. But after an extensive search they came away empty-handed.

"Snakeboot, I think you're wrong this time," said Al, feeling deflated. "There's nothing hidden in this room." He began to walk towards the door, but Snakeboot raced ahead of him and leapt into the doorway, arching his back and hissing.

"He sure doesn't want us to leave," said Jack. "Do you want us to search even more, Snakeboot?"

The cat purred in answer.

"Well, as they say, leave no stone unturned," replied Al. "Let's find a chair, climb up and push at the ceiling. Then we'll tap the floorboards."

Late in the afternoon, Jack found a loose board, pulled it up, and discovered an old cardboard box. Inside was a slip of paper with the word 'geranium' written on it.

"It could be a secret word," said Al. "Sometimes there are coded messages that can't be solved unless you have a secret word." He turned to find that Snakeboot was already leaving the room, so they followed him down the stairs.

The cat stopped in the storeroom.

"I think we've got to search the whole warehouse now," moaned Jack. "For a message."

"There may be a pattern," said Al. "As we found this secret word under a loose floorboard, I reckon we should begin with the floors."

After hours of careful tapping and lifting, Al discovered a loose board under the stairwell. He prised it up and discovered another small box containing a piece of paper with the letters 'fkkd tjanp smn pna

ufgqq wbjakw' written on it.

"This is definitely a coded message," said Al. "Now all we have to do is work out what it says." He wrote 'geranium' in the dust and then wrote the rest of the alphabet after it. As he already knew about secret word codes, he had the message deciphered in no time.

"Did any of you notice a red window?" he asked.

The other boys shook their heads.

"The message says 'look under the red glass window'," said Al, baffled. He ran back up the stairs and into the many empty office rooms, but there wasn't even a red trim on any of the windows. Just as he was about to give up, he noticed the glass in the windows on the western wall glowing red in the setting sun.

He searched and quickly found a loose brick and, pulling it from the wall, reached inside the wall cavity. There he found a gold jewellery box. Inside were several large, uncut emeralds.

"This must have been part of Prince Alleric's treasure!" said Al excitedly. "I wonder if it'll be enough to win the bid for the Dragon Blood Sabre and Scabbard of Invisibility at the auction?"

"It'll depend on how many people are bidding against us," Jack replied. "But there's enough treasure here to give it a go."

On Wednesday morning, Snotty Nell was surprised to see the boys at the auction and Grenda couldn't contain her smile when Al began to compete for his magical weapons. He was very lucky, because many people hadn't believed Stanley Spong could possibly have found the real sabre and scabbard, and had thought the auction a scam. Those who did believe were few and far between, and although their bids went high, they couldn't beat Al's emeralds. Soon, he had won!

In ten minutes the sabre and scabbard were once again in Al's hands and he proudly strapped them to his waist. Snotty's eye glittered with joy as she took the gold jewellery box and went off with a spring in her step to buy a new boat on the wharf.

Return of Blacktooth

Half an hour after the auction, Blacktooth's
ship, *The Tyrant*, docked. Its hold was filled
with gold and the pirate was looking forward
to a big spend-up.

Within minutes of swaggering ashore,
however, Blacktooth heard that the Dragon
Blood Sabre and Scabbard of Invincibility
had just been sold at auction to three boys.

Blacktooth couldn't believe his ears.

"If we'd docked an hour earlier," he said to himself, "those beautiess'd be mine!"

Blacktooth wasted no time in finding out that the boys were holed up in the old Alleric Warehouse, and, with a band of his cut-throats, he set off to find them.

Al, Jack and Mahoot had returned from the auction feeling very pleased with themselves. They were sitting down in the warehouse enjoying some cakes they had bought from the baker in exchange for some booty. "I've got one emerald left," said Al, holding the gem out for his friends to see. "It's one of the bigger ones. It'll buy us a passage to Sabre Island."

"Perhaps your grandfather would let us live there for a while until we work out what to do next," said Jack.

"And with Snakeboot's help we could look for more treasure in Alleric Castle," said Mahoot, getting excited about returning home.

"I wonder where Gunner is?" said Al. "I can't work out how he could have lost the sabre and scabbard to Snotty. His boat is fast. Maybe he got wrecked."

"Maybe Blacktooth sank him," said Jack.

"But then Blacktooth would have the sabre," said Al.

"Blacktooth hass it now!" shouted Blacktooth,

leaping through the warehouse door with his gang of pirates behind him.

Snakeboot sprang towards the door, hissing, and, with all claws drawn, attacked Pigface McNurt, Blacktooth's bosun. Pigface drew his sword and savagely slashed at the cat. The blow sent Snakeboot flying into a wall, and he fell to the ground, unmoving.

Al leapt to his feet, drew his sabre and raced over to Snakeboot. Blood trickled into the dust from a large gash along the cat's side. Furious, Al turned to face his enemy.

Blacktooth signalled and the pirates surrounded Al with drawn swords.

Blacktooth's cabin boy, Flash, strutted up to him. "Give us your sabre," he said with a cocky grin. "Give up now before we kill you."

"You can't touch me and you know it," Al replied.

"We can't touch you," Blacktooth growled,

"but we can touch them!" He pointed at Jack and Mahoot.

Pigface grabbed Mahoot by the arm and held his sword's razor-sharp point to his throat.

"We'll jusst kill your friendss," threatened Blacktooth. "You don't want to ssee them die, do you? Sso sstop being a ssilly ssilt-head and hand over your weaponss."

Jack, who was further back in the room, made a break for the door, but one of the pirates leapt after him and tackled him to the ground.

"I wouldn't try anything," hissed Flash. He spat at Al's feet. "Give me the sabre." He held out his hand.

"He'll give it to *me*!" Blacktooth corrected. "I'm sstill the captain!"

Flash reddened. "You said we'd be co-captains," he grumbled. "I'm the one who found all the treasure on Velvetfoot's Island."

Blacktooth fixed Flash a dark scowl. "Enough!" he thundered. "We'll ssort thiss out back on the boat." He turned to Al. "Hand me that ssabre or your friendss will sstart sscreaming."

"Start by cutting off their ears!" ordered Flash.

"Stop!" cried Al. "Here!" He unbuckled the sabre and held it out. "No treasure is worth one of my friends being hurt."

"You ssee," said Blacktooth, holding the sword high, "I deserve thiss. You gave it up too eassily. I'm not afraid to kill to get it, and I'm not worried if ssomeone diess sso I can keep it. This ssabre will be mine for the resst of my life."

He grinned evilly, showing his one black tooth. "And I'll live for ever, becausse I'm never taking the sscabbard off!"

"Can we get rid of them now?" interrupted Flash, glaring at Al and his friends with hatred.

Blacktooth looked around the warehouse. "There'ss lotss of folk who ssaw us come in here," he said. "There'ss an unsspoken pirate code: we can't do murderss in town. We have to abide by that rule or we can't come back."

"So what will we do with them?" asked Flash.

"I've got a far better idea," smiled Blacktooth. "We'll take them ssailing."

Blacktooth marched Al, Jack and Mahoot back to *The Tyrant*, cast off with haste and set sail.

Once out at sea, he tied the boys' arms and legs together and, several hours later, lowered them over the side of the ship and left them on a small rock in the middle of the ocean.

"The tide'ss going out now!" he called.
"You've got twelve hourss before Greeny
Joe getss you for dinner." He laughed
uproariously and waved the Dragon Blood
Sabre. The ruby in the hilt glowed blood-red
in the sunlight.

Guilt

While Blacktooth was leading the boys away from the warehouse, Snakeboot, who was lying mortally wounded on the floor, shimmered, became transparent and vanished. Only a small pool of blood remained.

Seconds later, Snakeboot appeared at his old home on Ghost Island, inside the treasure vault of Vicious Victor, the pirate ghost. The cat shook himself, meowed and jumped joyfully into the lap of the skeletal remains of the pirate.

Snakeboot's arrival stirred Victor's rotting bones. His toothy jaw shook in delight and his disembodied voice shivered through the air. "Snakeboot! It's been ages since you've visited me." He patted his old friend and then, noticing the blood on the animal's fur, said, "I see you've used up one of your nine lives, old puss. Well, you've come to the right place to get better. Rest here a minute or two and let Ghost Island fix you with its powers, then you must go back and finish what we began."

Holding the cat in his arms, Vicious Victor stood up and began pacing the treasure vault, his bones rattling. He sighed. "I'm still stuck here! It's been my prison for nearly one hundred years. Snakeboot, I'm tired of feeling guilty about all the wrongs I've committed. I'm tired of talking to myself. I'm depending on you to fix the problems that are keeping me here. I can't rest in peace until those boys

have found all of Alleric's lost treasure. You must continue to help them."

As Vicious Victor patted Snakeboot, the bleeding gash closed over, and only a fresh pink scar remained. Victor put the cat back on the floor. "Now be gone!" he said. "Go back, find the boys and finish our work."

The cat purred in reply, shimmered, became ghostly and disappeared.

After Snotty Nell left the anchorage, Captain Gunner went to bed and slept soundly until a clap of thunder woke him in the morning. He leapt up, looked out of the cabin at the darkening thunderheads, dressed and, to his horror, discovered the sabre and scabbard missing.

Realising that Snotty must have stolen them, he grabbed his old iron sword and leapt onto the deck, shouting, "Hoist the sails! Hurry! Hurry! We've got to get Snotty!"

But just as he raised his sword, a lightning bolt burst from the sky. It hit Gunner's sword, ripping it from his hand and burning his arm. With his hair standing on end, Gunner let out a shriek of terror and leapt around the poop deck in agony. Fearing their captain had gone mad and they were about to be attacked by devils, the crew ran to the sails and pulled anchor faster than ever before.

The wind against them, *The Invincible* made slow progress and was buffeted so badly that Gunner had to reef down his sails. Worse, the storm had lashed the sea into a fury, so the lookout didn't see a log floating in their path. *The Invincible* rammed into it, making it jam against the rudder, bending its pin. Gunner suddenly found himself sailing ten degrees off the breeze. He was forced to come about more often and his journey was slowed further. Then he discovered that the lightning bolt had destroyed his perfectly good compass, which had caused him to overshoot the town and sail past it by a day.

"It's a punishment upon me," Gunner moaned. "I've broken pirate law and nothing will help me until I fix what I've done." He cradled his burnt arm and groaned in pain. "I doubt those boys are ever gunner trust me again."

Finally Gunner managed to dock in town beside a fishing boat, which was unloading its daily catch. The fishnet was rigged from the boat's boom and, as it swung towards the dock, a rope holding the net snapped. The entire cargo of fish fell onto *The Invincible's* poop deck and all over Captain Gunner.

...h, his hair frizzed, his burnt
...is melted sword useless, his
...troyed, his rudder bent and
his ... on Blacktooth ruined, Gunner
slumped to the deck in misery.

But Mozzy, realising the boat was doomed
until the pirate's curse was lifted, wasted no time
and sent the crew ashore to search for the boys.

Several minutes later Slicer returned with
the news that the boys had bought the sabre
and scabbard at an auction and had been seen
going to sea with Blacktooth.

"It's all my fault," wailed Gunner, sinking
further into despair. "Blacktooth's bound to
kill them. He hates those boys. Woe is me.
What will I do?"

In answer, a white cat with purple eyes
leapt onto his shoulder and dug its claws into
his arm.

"Ow!" Gunner yelled. "What was that for,
Snakeboot? Can't you see I'm a destroyed

man? I've done the boys down and I'm
gunner pay for it for all eternity!"

Snakeboot let out a mighty yowl and ran
to the bow, where he howled and howled.
Then he ran back to Gunner and jumped
back on his shoulder.

"All right!" exclaimed Gunner. "I get it.
You want me to go to sea. I've got nothing
to lose, so I'm gunner follow you."

Once again Gunner set sail and, as his
crew cleaned the boat and threw the fish into
the sea, he followed Snakeboot's directions
as he scampered from port to starboard with
accompanying yowls.

Al, Jack and Mahoot wriggled as far up
the rock as they possibly could. Then they
worked at untying each other, but as they
did so the tide came in. Finally, just as they
were free, Al spotted the giant green fin of a
familiar shark.

"Greeny Joe's here!" said Al, rubbing the life back into his arms. "This is just like the first time we came to the Dragon Blood Islands. It's the same rock and the same shark come to eat us!"

"Except there's no magical cat arriving to save us," said Jack.

"We could try howling," said Mahoot, paling at the sight of the giant shark so close.

"How long do you think we've got?" said Jack.

"No more than two hours," said Al, glancing at the sun.

"What's that?" said Mahoot.

"What's what?" said Al and Jack at the same time.

"Shhh!" said Mahoot. "Listen."

In the distance they heard the faint yowling of a cat.

"Snakeboot!" cheered the boys. "Snnnaaaakkkeeboooooooot!"

Soon afterwards, they sighted a sail on the horizon.

Sea Battle

Al and Jack sat on the docks in town with Snakeboot curled up between them. Gunner was supervising the repair to the rudder and Mozzy was loading more gunpowder and cannonballs.

"We'll sail by tomorrow morning," said Mahoot. "Gunner's still feeling so guilty he's barely slept since he rescued us."

"I've never seen him so, well, unlike Gunner," said Jack. "He's spent every last bit of his treasure getting those cannons and he

plans to hunt Blacktooth down. For once
I think he may succeed."

Al patted Snakeboot.
"I can't believe how lucky
we were," he said. "Who'd
have thought Snakeboot
could recover like he
did? I know he's sort
of ghostly and magical,
but I really thought he
was dead." He tickled
Snakeboot's ear. "And
I'm so glad you aren't.
You saved us again!"

The Invincible set sail the following morning
and Gunner voiced his plan.

"I know Blacktooth will be in the waters
somewhere off Velvetfoot's Island. He wants
to build a fort there, so I'm gunner hunt him
down and blow him out of the water."

"He won't give up the sabre and scabbard," said Al. "He can fight you and not be injured at all."

"If he's in the water, it'll be different," said Gunner. "We might not be able to kill him, but he can't swim. Eventually he'll have to trade with us."

"It's a good plan," Al agreed. "But we have to find him first."

A few days later they spotted *The Tyrant* off the port side. Gunner ordered full sail and commanded everyone to battle stations. He persuaded Al, Mahoot and Jack to go below and provide first aid if needed.

The Tyrant's crew, realising they were about to be attacked, hoisted the Jolly Roger and the ship came about, preparing to meet the enemy.

The Invincible bore down and fired a broadside. The combination of the giant guns, the smell of gunpowder and the cheers from the men announced that their first attack had reached its target.

Blacktooth's flag and topsail vanished in a puff of vapour. Hailstorms of splinters and razor-edged debris swept over his decks from the demolition. Blacktooth, realising the long-range cannons would finish him off quickly, came about and headed straight for *The Invincible*, trying to get underneath the fire. He closed in, cannons and muskets blasting, keen to ram Gunner amidships.

Gunner, at the helm, steered away, avoiding the collision.

As both boats fired mercilessly at each other, the air filled with smoke so thick that nobody could see beyond the length of their ship. Below decks the smoking cannons choked the air and stung the boys' eyes, and the continual manoeuvring and tacking had them constantly off-balance. But Gunner

made good use of the wind and put a
broadside into *The Tyrant*.

Blacktooth fired back, one of his cannons
blasting into the wheelhouse, nearly killing
Gunner in a spray of splinters and metal.
Wiping blood from his brow and nursing
one hand that was bleeding heavily, Gunner
called for another cannon blast.

"We'll never yield!" he shouted. "We're getting back what's ours!"

Outgunned, Blacktooth turned and ran before the breeze, hoping to escape *The Invincible*. He fired one last broadside and blew a hole near one of Gunner's long-range cannons, right beside where the boys were working. *The Invincible*'s pirates

were thrown to the decks by the force of
the explosion. Al and Jack pulled the injured
men to one side, and Mahoot ran for
bandages and hot tar to staunch their
terrible wounds.

Gunner blasted back at *The Tyrant*, hitting
it below deck, blowing up Blacktooth's
powder magazine and sending men flying.
Fire broke out and surged upwards in a
crackling roar.

"They've had it!" cried Gunner, spying Blacktooth standing at the prow, immune to the flames.

Realising his boat was damaged beyond repair, Blacktooth ran for the poop deck and made ready to lower the longboat. Gunner fired again, this time at closer range. The longboat exploded across the deck in a hail of splinters, killing several pirates around Blacktooth but leaving him unscathed.

"You'll not get me!" Blacktooth bellowed.

Gunner fired again and this time the main mast fell. Spars and sails crashed down, burying Blacktooth in a tangle of canvas and rigging. Pigface McNurt, Flash and several other pirates raced to the treasure-hold to salvage their booty just as the timber hull split open. Suddenly the boat foundered and they found themselves trapped in an air pocket. As none of them could swim they panicked. When they realised that the more men sharing the limited air inside the hull, the less time each would have to live, they turned on each other. Finally, *The Tyrant* rolled, throwing men into the water.

Blacktooth, wrapped tightly from head to foot in sailcloth and ropes, was dragged underwater. After several seconds of blind panic, his lungs bursting and his eyes popping, he was forced to take a breath. But instead of drowning, he discovered that he was able to breathe. The magical scabbard

had given him unearthly powers of survival. As he wriggled, trying to escape, he realised he was wrapping himself more firmly in *The Tyrant*'s ropes. His arms and legs were bound so tightly that he couldn't reach the sabre to cut himself free.

The joy of being invincible soon wore off and Blacktooth realised that although he couldn't die as long as he wore the scabbard, his boat would still sink and pull him down to Davey Jones' Locker, where he'd stay with the eels and fishes until the rigging rotted. The thought made him very scared and angry at the same time. "By then," he raged, "that Flash will have spent all my treasure!"

Saving Blacktooth's Pirates

Battle over, the boys emerged on deck. Captain Gunner had already attached a grappling line to *The Tyrant* and pulled her alongside *The Invincible*. The shouts and blows of metal upon metal from the submerged hold made the boys shudder.

"We must try to save them," said Al. "We can't leave them like that. Jack, Mahoot and

I must dive down and help them to the surface."

"You could also get your head cut off," said Gunner sarcastically.

But Al couldn't stand it any longer so, without asking Gunner's permission, he grabbed hold of a line and, hand over hand, monkeyed down to *The Tyrant*'s upturned hull.

Jack and Mahoot followed. Minutes later, holding one end of a long rope, Al dived.

He swam down to a gaping hole in *The Tyrant*'s side and bravely swam through and then upwards until he found a small air pocket. He gathered his breath and gave the rope two tugs, which told Jack and Mahoot he was fine. Then he took a deep breath and dived again, swimming down a companionway, following the noise made by the pirates.

With his lungs bursting and the rope almost at its end, Al managed to surface inside the cabin where everyone was trapped.

His arrival startled the warring pirates into

silence. Flash, his face bleeding, stared at his enemy in disbelief. His face paled.

"A ghost!" screamed Pigface. "We're being punished by a ghost!" He splashed to the back and cowered behind a wounded shipmate who he had been trying to kill only seconds before.

"I'm no ghost," said Al. "We were rescued, and I've come to help you." He held out the rope. "Instead of fighting each other, use your energy to take a deep breath and pull yourselves hand over hand along this rope. It'll lead you to the surface."

Pigface needed no further instruction. He leapt to the rope, took a huge breath and dragged himself down. One by one the surviving pirates followed his lead. Finally, Flash turned to Al. "I don't know how you keep popping up. But you're here, so maybe I should do the job properly and kill you once and for all!" He raised his sword.

"But if I don't get back to *The Invincible*, Gunner will kill you," said Al. "How would that help?"

"You've got less brains than a sea lice," growled Flash, realising he had to accept Al's help. "You're the dumbest pirate I've ever met." He grabbed the safety rope and hauled himself ungraciously down into the water.

When the rope stopped shaking, Al knew Flash was safe so he pulled hard on it three times. Jack and Mahoot felt the tug and began hauling Al to the surface.

Once all of Blacktooth's remaining pirates were tied up and safely stowed as prisoners, Gunner scratched his chin, deep in thought. He stared at the water and the upturned Tyrant. "Blacktooth's still down there somewhere," he said, "but how are we gunner find him?"

"We'll keep looking, at least until the

boat sinks," said Al. As he spoke, there was a whoosh of trapped air and the upturned boat shifted thirty degrees. The poop deck and the tangle of ropes and sails became visible in the clear waters below.

"He's trapped in there for sure," said Jack. "How about we go down and feel around? If we find him, we'll work out what to do."

Mahoot was the first to find the wriggling cocoon of sail with Blacktooth snared inside. He swam back up and pointed him out to Al, who took a knife and made the next dive. Carefully, he cut around Blacktooth's waist, exposing the scabbard. He put his hand on the treasure. How easy it would be, he thought, to cut through the belt and take both the sabre and the scabbard and leave Blacktooth to his fate. But Al was better than that; he was no murderer.

Rapidly running out of air, Al dared to put his hand on the scabbard.

I hope it can make us both invincible, Al
thought. He shut his eyes and breathed. To his
delight the sheath protected him.

Making sure the scabbard was touching
Blacktooth at all times, he cut it away
from the pirate's body, and cut the ropes
and sailcloth from around his face, until
Blacktooth was able to see him. Al signalled
that he was going to release Blacktooth's arms

from their bindings and, with both of them holding the sabre and scabbard, they would surface together.

Blacktooth nodded in agreement, so Al went ahead, allowing him to hold one end of the scabbard.

Suddenly, Blacktooth grabbed Al by his hair, wrenched the boy's head up and at the same time pulled down hard on the scabbard.

In shock, Al dropped his knife and lost his grip on the sheath. He struggled to regain his hold, but no matter how hard he fought, Blacktooth kept his murderous grip on Al and the scabbard out of reach.

As the oxygen left Al's body, lights danced before his eyes. With his lungs bursting, he realised he was going to die.

From above, Jack and Mahoot watched the battle in the water. Realising their friend was about to be killed, they grabbed weapons and were ready to plunge into the sea when, to their horror, a large green torpedo shot through the water beneath them.

"Greeeeny Joe!" screamed Gunner in warning. He immediately ordered his pirates to fire their muskets at the beast, but the water deflected their shots, and the dreaded shark went for his lunch.

Just as Al, with the last of his strength, made a desperate attempt to grab the scabbard, Blacktooth released him. Al managed to seize the flashing silver sheath and his strength returned to him in seconds. He focused. Greeny Joe's enormous body was only centimetres from his own, and Blacktooth was firmly between the shark's jaws.

Al's eyes widened in horror as Greeny Joe circled down into the dark ocean below and disappeared.

Playing Pirates

With the Dragon Blood Sabre and Scabbard
of Invincibility back in Al's hands, Gunner
headed for Velvetfoot's treasure island. "I'm
really sorry for what I put you boys through,"
he said. "I wrecked everything and I don't
deserve your trust. If it helps, though, we
now have Velvetfoot's treasure as our own.
Blacktooth won't be needing it, and Flash
is our prisoner. We could fill our holds with
booty and take it to Sabre Island. I know
you want to restore Alleric Castle and help

Grandfather look after all the animals in the jungle."

Days later, the boys found themselves in Velvetfoot's cave. Following Gunner's lead, Al and Jack loaded a chest with gold doubloons, and Mahoot took several small sacks of jewels.

Hoisting the heavy chest between them, the boys followed the treasure-laden pirates back to *The Invincible*. The chest was much heavier than the boys realised so they had to stop for breath and put it down.

"I reckon there's lots more Alleric treasure still lost out there," said Jack, puffing slightly. "Am I right, Snakeboot?"

The cat purred in answer.

Suddenly Al's fingers began to tingle. He looked across at Jack, who was fading from his sight.

"We're going home," Al said.

Seconds later, he was standing in his attic at number five Drake Drive in the twenty-first century. Jack was beside him and Snakeboot was sitting on the sea trunk's lid.

Just as Al unbuckled his sabre and scabbard and carefully put them back on the top of an old cupboard, the attic door opened and

Al's dad stuck his head inside.

"There you are!" he said. "Didn't you hear me calling?"

Al shook his head. "We were playing."

"Playing pirates," said his dad, smiling at their pirate clothes. "Al, you're just like your grandfather. He was always telling me bedtime stories about pirates. He had all these insane stories about a nasty pirate called Vitriolic Victor and some place called Sword Island."

"You mean Vicious Victor and Sabre Island?" asked Al.

"Yes, that was it," said his dad. "How did you know?"

"Did he say there were elephants on Sabre Island?" asked Jack.

"He did!" replied Al's dad. "Swimming elephants. One day I came up here to the attic and found my father standing in that old sea trunk over there, dressed as a pirate. It was really embarrassing having a father playing pirates, I can tell you. You're very lucky I don't do things like that."

"Did he say anything about the sea trunk?" asked Al hopefully.

"Some nonsense about how his own

grandfather had it made by a sorcerer, or perhaps it was his grandfather who was the sorcerer," said Al's dad. "I forget. I do remember he tried to tell me he'd just been to an abandoned underground city to look for some magic words to make the trunk work properly. Who'd believe that?" Al's dad chuckled as he left the attic, closing the door behind him.

With that, the boys sensed movement behind them and turned to see the sabre plunging into the floorboards. As it came to a standstill, the blade glinted before them.

Wide-eyed, Al and Jack exchanged a look. They still had work to do in the Dragon Blood Islands.

Captain's Code

To solve the puzzle on pages 44 and 45,
first write down the code word 'geranium',
and then write out the remaining letters
of the alphabet in order. This is your new
'alphabet'. The letters of the standard
alphabet are now represented by the letters
of the new alphabet, and you should be able
to decipher the coded message.
If you need help, dare to visit
www.dragonbloodpirates.co.uk

Arrr! Ahoy there, mateys!

Hoist the sails and drop the anchor: ye have some treasure to find!

One swashbucklin' reader will win an ipod Touch and ten runners up will win a Dragon Blood Pirates booty bag. For a chance to win, ye must dare to unearth the treasure!

Each of the six **Dragon Blood Pirates: The Legend of Dragon Island** books contain a clue. When you have solved the six clues, enter the answers online at www.dragonbloodpirates.co.uk

Or send your name, address and answers to:

Dragon Blood Pirates:
The Legend of Dragon Island
338 Euston Road, London NW1 3BH

Best o' luck, me hearties!

To find where the pirate treasure lies,
ye must find the answer to the clue that lies below:

**This pirate has come to the end of his time,
A shark ensures he can do no more crimes.**

Only one entry per child. Final draw 31 August 2011.
For full terms and conditions visit
www.dragonbloodpirates.co.uk/terms

www.dragonbloodpirates.co.uk

Ahoy there shipmates!

To reel in amazin' pirate booty, steer smartly
towards www.dragonbloodpirates.co.uk

Ye'll find games, downloads, activities and
sneak previews of the latest swashbucklin'
Dragon Blood Pirates adventures.
Learn how to speak all pirate-like, how to find
out what type of pirate ye be, an' what pirate
games ye can play with yer mates! This treasure
trove is a sure feast fer yer deadlights!

Only the bravest an' heartiest amon' ye
can become a true scurvy dog, so don't
ye miss a thing and sign up to yer newsletter
at www.dragonbloodpirates.co.uk!

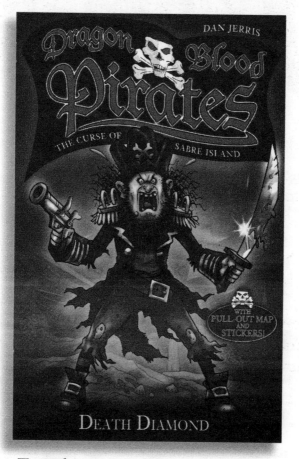

Prologue

Al Breas's arms tingled. His feet were wet. Bewildered, he opened his eyes and stared in shock. What was he doing on a rock in the middle of the ocean? Then his friend Jack Seabrook began to appear beside him, shimmering ghost-like for a moment before becoming solid.

Jack's eyes bugged in disbelief as he looked around. "Where *are* we?"

"I have no idea," Al said. He rubbed his

eyes. Only seconds ago he and Jack had been playing in his attic at number five Drake Drive. They'd been drinking cola and Al's dad had been yelling at him to come downstairs and do the dishes.

But Al hated doing chores, and besides, he'd been more interested in the big rusty key he'd just found. When he'd tried it in the lock of the old sea trunk that had once belonged to his grandfather, the mysterious chest had opened.

The sea trunk had been empty, but drawn onto the base was a map of some strange islands. The word **treasure** had leapt out at them, so Al and Jack had leant into the trunk to have a closer look. Suddenly, Al had felt his body go all odd and goosebumpy. He'd clutched the key in his hand and shut his eyes.

Now he was stuck with his best friend in the middle of the ocean on a small rocky outcrop!

"What's *that*?" Jack's eyes bugged out even further. Before them a white ghostly cat appeared. Within seconds the animal solidified just as Jack had done. Wobbling slightly on three legs, its weird purple eyes shone in the sunlight.

Then, apparently terrified, it leapt into Al's lap, mewing pitifully. Al put the rusty key in his pocket and patted the distressed creature.

The tide was coming in and waves swirled around the rock, close to their feet. There also seemed to be a strange green shadow in the water, circling slowly around them. Then a fin cut the surface and Al's eyes widened in fear. "Oh no!" he cried. "A shark!"

The giant creature was so close they could see its cold eyes glowing with menace and green phosphorous mould growing on its ancient skin.

"Help!" Jack and Al both screamed.

The frightened cat clung to Al's tracksuit bottoms and howled, its wail travelling far across the waters.

Just as the waves were lapping at their feet and the shark was sizing them up for dinner, Al and Jack saw a sail in the distance. To their relief, after a few minutes the ship sailed right up to them and dropped anchor.

"It looks like an old Christopher Columbus ship," said Al, waving frantically to the several scruffy men who peered down at them from the ship's rails.

"It's called *The Booty*," Jack spotted, as the ship's patched sails were hauled down and a lifeboat launched.

Seeing the monstrous green shark circling the rock, the men in the lifeboat beat the water with their paddles. The shark thrashed its tail and headed out to sea.

Al and Jack were rescued!

Pirates

"Maggoty biscuits?" said Al in disgust, staring at the plate set before him in the ship's galley.

"Don't you want your dinner?" asked a barefoot boy.

"No, thanks," said Jack.

A tattooed man wielding a knife leered at Jack and Al menacingly. "You'll be sorry," he said.

The barefoot boy grinned, picked up

one of the biscuits and bit into it hungrily.
"Don't take any notice of Slicer," he said.
"My name's Mahoot. I'm the cabin boy, and
let me tell you, there's not much food left.
We haven't found any treasure, you see."

"Treasure?" Al asked, bewildered.

"We've been sailing through the Dragon
Blood Islands for months now," said Mahoot.

"Nothing! But Captain Gunner did say our luck would change." He pointed to the three-legged cat, which now sat curled up in a corner of *The Booty*'s galley. "When we heard a strange howling, Captain Gunner followed the sound and we found you. I reckon if you hadn't had that furball with you, the captain would have left you there to be eaten by old Greeny Joe. This ship doesn't need two more mouths to feed, that's for sure."

"What's so important about the cat?" Al asked.

"Snakeboot's a sea-going cat," Slicer replied. He reached out and tickled the cat under the chin.

"Snakeboot?" said Jack.

"There's this legend," explained Mahoot. "A cat exactly like yours belonged to a famous pirate called Vicious Victor, who died ages ago. A snake bit the cat and the cat chewed its own leg off rather than die from the poison. So Vicious Victor called it Snakeboot."

"A pirate's cat?" said Jack.

"With a cat like that," said Slicer, "we'll get lucky and rich. *And* he'll keep the rats down."

No sooner had Slicer spoken than a strong wind howled through the rigging and *The Booty* rolled to one side. The plates on the table clattered to the floor.

"Storm approaching!" screamed the bosun from above.

"We'd better find you a place to bunk down," said Mahoot. "The storms around here can be fierce. And you boys don't look like you have your sea legs yet."

The storm raged and the ship rolled and pitched. The boys sheltered in the dank hold, which stank of sewage and rats. Between stomach-heaving swells and violent seasickness, Jack peered at Al with red-rimmed eyes and said, "I want to go home."

Al agreed, but there was nothing they could do. They were stuck on a ship with what appeared to be pirates, in a place called the Dragon Blood Islands...

Death Island

When the tossing seas quietened, Al and Jack made their way unsteadily to the deck. Al squinted in the sunlight and looked around. *The Booty* was anchored in a cove, and cliffs towered above them.

The storm had wreaked havoc on the ship. The torn mainsail lay on the deck, tattered ropes were jumbled in piles and seawater sloshed in the scuppers. Captain Gunner, his black frock coat ripped and his pantaloons gaping at the knee, strode up and down the deck, inspecting the damage. His gaze fell on the boys as they emerged from the hold. "You hopeless little landlubbers!" he bawled. "Come here!"

Al and Jack did as they were told.

"The salt water's got into the biscuits, so there's no food," said Captain Gunner. "You good-for-nothings will have to earn your

keep while we fix the ship." He handed the boys two balls of string with hooks on the ends. "Now catch us some fish."

On top of the cliffs nearby, coconut palms waved in the breeze. "Couldn't we go ashore instead and get some fruit?" Al asked.

Captain Gunner took a step back, his face pale. "That's Death Island. No one goes there. Now get to work or I'm gunner feed you to Greeny Joe."

Al and Jack hung maggoty biscuits from the fish-hooks. But the fish swam by without a glance.

Jack's stomach rumbled loudly. "I'm starving," he said.

Al surveyed the island nearby. With its banana trees and coconuts, he guessed it would bear enough food for all of them. He spied a cave at the foot of the cliffs. Then he looked at *The Booty*'s dinghy. "We could take their dinghy, go through that cave and get some food," he said excitedly.

"I wouldn't if I were you." The boys jumped. They hadn't seen Mahoot come up behind them. "No one who's gone through that cave has ever returned," he told them. "That's why it's called Death Island…"